THE GA...

ROCKIN' REPTILES

by **Stephanie Calmenson** and **Joanna Cole**

illustrated by **Lynn Munsinger**

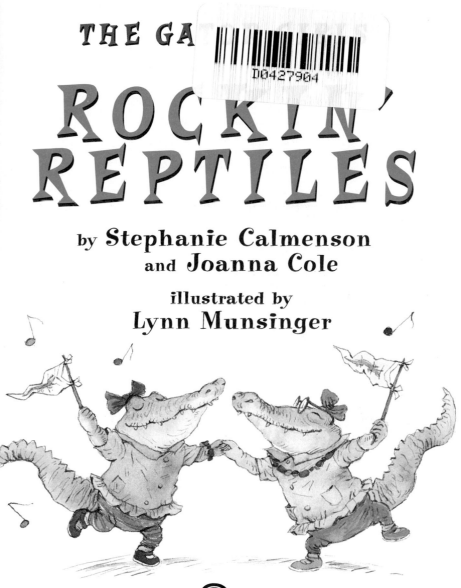

Beech Tree
New York

Pen and ink with watercolor was used for the full-color illustrations.
The text type is 18-point Palatino.

The Library of Congress has cataloged the Morrow Junior Books
edition of *Rockin' Reptiles* as follows:
Calmenson, Stephanie.
Rockin' reptiles/by Stephanie S. Calmenson and Joanna Cole;
illustrated by Lynn Munsinger.
p. cm.—(The Gator Girls)
Summary: Because the new girl on the block has only
one extra ticket for the most exciting concert ever,
two best friends must decide which of them gets to go.
ISBN 0-688-12739-8 (trade)—ISBN 0-688-12740-1 (library)
[1. Friendship—Fiction. 2. Alligators—Fiction.] I. Cole, Joanna.
II. Munsinger, Lynn, ill. III. Title. IV. Series: Calmenson, Stephanie.
Gator Girls. PZ7.C136Ro 1997 [Fic]—dc20 96–16067 CIP AC

First Beech Tree Edition, 1998
ISBN 0-688-15633-9
10 9 8 7 6 5 4 3 2 1

Reprinted by arrangement with William Morrow & Company, Inc.

CONTENTS

1 · RING! RING! / 5

2 · NEW GATOR ON THE BLOCK / 11

3 · SOLD OUT! / 17

4 · GRACIE CALLING / 26

5 · WHO WILL BE
THE LUCKY GATOR? / 37

6 · LOOK WHO'S NOT TALKING / 45

7 · THE CRYSTAL BALL HAS SPOKEN / 53

8 · WHAT TO DO? / 62

9 · ROCKIN' REPTILES! / 72

1
RING! RING!

Ring! Ring! Early one morning the telephone rang at Allie Gator's house. Allie's father answered it.

"It's for you, Allie!" he called. "It's Amy."

"I knew that!" said Allie. She jumped out of bed and ran for the phone.

Allie and Amy were best friends. They lived in apartment buildings next door to each other. When they were not together, they were talking on the phone.

"Quick, look out your window," said Amy. "Look what it says on that truck outside."

Allie looked out. "I can't read it," she said. "I don't have my glasses on."

"It says Moving Van. And look what they're unloading," said Amy.

"I can't see it. Everything is fuzzy," said Allie.

"Please put your glasses on. This is important!" said Amy.

Allie ran and put on her glasses. She looked out the window.

She saw the movers taking a bed out of the truck. On the headboard, in big letters, it said GRACIE. A bulletin board resting on the sidewalk said GRACIE, too. So did the toy chest.

"It looks like a girl is moving into your building," said Amy.

"I wonder what her name is," said Allie.

"Very funny," said Amy. "Hurry up and get ready. I'll meet you downstairs."

As Allie jumped into her clothes, her head was swimming with questions. I wonder if Gracie is nice. I wonder if she likes jumping rope.

As she gobbled down her breakfast, she thought, I wonder if she likes the Rockin' Reptiles band. I wonder if she eats dragonfly pizza.

Allie raced for the elevator. She lived on the sixth floor of her building. She pressed the button for the first floor. The floor numbers lit up. *Six, five, four, three, two, one.*

Amy lived on the sixth floor of *her* building. At the very same time as Allie, she pressed the button for the first floor. *Six, five, four, three, two, one.*

Allie and Amy burst out of their doors together. The movers were taking more and more stuff out of the van.

Just then a car pulled up to the curb. Behind the wheel was a lady alligator. A skinny alligator girl was sitting next to her. She had braces on her teeth. Her T-shirt had big letters across the front. The letters spelled out GRACIE.

The girl opened the car door and jumped out.

"Hi. I'm Gracie," she said.

"Oh, really?" said Allie, trying not to laugh.

"Be nice," whispered Amy to Allie. She turned to Gracie and said, "Hi. I'm Amy, and this is Allie. Welcome to Swamp Street."

2
NEW GATOR
ON THE BLOCK

The movers carried a trampoline out of the truck and rested it on the sidewalk.

"Ooh, that looks like fun," said Allie.

"Want to try it?" asked Gracie.

"Sure," Allie said, kicking off her shoes.

She stepped onto the trampoline. *Boing, boing, boing!* She went up and down and up and down.

"My turn!" said Amy. *Boing, boing, boing.*

It was Gracie's turn next. *Boing, boing, boing.* While she was jumping, the movers came by, carrying a basketball hoop. Gracie stopped jumping.

"Please wait! We need that," called Gracie. She turned to Allie and Amy. "Want to play basketball?" she asked.

Before Allie and Amy could answer, Gracie disappeared into the truck. She came out with the basketball. *Ka-boom, ka-boom, ka-boom.* She bounced the ball to the basketball hoop and aimed. *Swish!* The ball dropped through the net.

"Yay! Two points!" said Gracie.

"My turn," said Amy. She threw the ball and missed. She threw again. *Swish!* This time she made a basket.

Allie caught the ball and threw it. *Swish!*

"Nice shot!" said Gracie. "I love basketball!" Allie tossed the ball to Gracie. Gracie bounced it under one leg, then the other.

"Want to hear a basketball riddle?" she said. "What do you get when you cross a stone with a basketball?"

"We don't know. What?" said Allie and Amy.

"Rock 'n' roll!" said Gracie, giggling. She dribbled the ball really fast in a circle, first around Allie, then Amy. *Ka-boom, ka-boom, ka-boom.*

While she was dribbling, a mover came by, carrying a lamp.

"Want to hear a lamp joke?" said Gracie. "Why did the lamp go on a diet?"

"Because it was too fat?" said Allie.

"Because its shade was too tight?" said Amy.

"No! Because it wanted to be lighter!" said Gracie.

The three of them were laughing when Gracie's mother called, "It's time to come inside!"

"Maybe we can play later," said Gracie. She dribbled and bounced all the way into the building.

3
SOLD OUT!

"Gracie's fun," said Amy. "She tells good jokes."

"She sure knows how to bounce that basketball," said Allie.

"She's pretty bouncy herself," said Amy.

Allie and Amy started walking down the block to the candy store.

"Look!" said Amy. She pointed to a big sign posted on a tree. It said:

There was a phone number to call for tickets.

"Wow! Our favorite group," cried Allie. "Maybe we can go to the concert."

They started to sing a Rockin' Reptiles hit song. It was called "Gotta Getta Gator."

I gotta getta gator to love me!
I gotta getta gator to hug me.
I gotta getta gator—
Now is better than la-ter!

Allie and Amy knew all the words. They flipped their tails in time to the music just the way the Rockin' Reptiles did.

They were starting on the second verse when an orange-haired alligator pulled up to the curb on a motorcycle. She walked up to the tree and slapped a sticker over the Rockin' Reptiles concert sign. It said:

Allie and Amy stopped in the middle of a high note and stared at the sign.

"I can't believe it. We can't go!" said Allie.

Vrooom. The motorcycle started pulling away.

"Wait!" Amy called. "Are you sure it's sold out? We just need two tickets."

But the orange-haired alligator did not hear.

"There must be a way to get tickets," Allie said to Amy. "We just have to think hard."

Whoosh! An alligator whizzed by on a skateboard. *Whoosh!* He whizzed back in the other direction.

It was goony Marvin. Sometimes the Gator Girls had a good time with Marvin. But most of the time they thought he was the most obnoxious alligator ever.

"MARVIN!!! You almost ran over my tail!" said Allie.

"Almost doesn't count. I better try again," said Marvin.

Whoosh! On the way back, Marvin saw the concert sign.

"Wow, the tickets are all sold out," he said. "I'm glad I already got mine."

"Do you mean that you—goony Marvin— have tickets to the Rockin' Reptiles concert?" asked Allie.

"I sure do," said Marvin. "Don't you?"

"Not yet," said Amy.

"You mean not *ever*," said Marvin. He started singing to the tune of "Gotta Getta Gator," "I've gotta buncha tickets...and you don't!"

"You are so obnoxious, Mr. Marvin Q. Smarty-pants," said Allie. "We do not associate with obnoxious alligators, do we, Amy?"

"No, we do not," said Amy.

The Gator Girls stood up, put their noses in the air, and stomped home. Marvin passed them on his skateboard several times, humming every Rockin' Reptiles tune he knew.

"I can't believe Marvin has tickets and we don't," said Allie when they reached their buildings.

"Me neither. It's not fair," said Amy.

"See you later, alligator," said Allie.

24

"In a while, crocodile," said Amy.

They went into their buildings humming another Reptiles hit song. It was called "Even Green Gators Get the Blues."

4
GRACIE CALLING

Ring! Ring! A few days later the phone rang at Allie's house.

"I'll get it!" called Allie to her mother. "Maybe it's Amy. Maybe she got tickets."

Allie picked up the phone and said like a radio announcer, "Rockin' Reptiles headquarters!"

"May I speak to Allie?" said a voice.

Oops. It wasn't Amy's voice.

"Who is this?" asked Allie.

"It's Gracie, your new neighbor," said the voice. "Do you want to come over? I got a new jewelry-making set. We could make necklaces and bracelets."

"I love making jewelry. Can Amy come, too?" asked Allie.

"I only have enough beads for two of us," said Gracie.

"Then I'm not sure…," said Allie. She was trying to decide if she should go without Amy.

"We'll have fun," said Gracie. "I have all kinds of beads. Round ones, square ones. Red ones, purple ones…"

"Purple's my favorite!" said Allie.

"The purple beads have silver sparkles," said Gracie.

"I'm on my way!" said Allie.

She zipped out the door and up one flight. Gracie lived in the apartment right over Allie's.

"I've got everything ready," said Gracie, leading Allie to her room. The jewelry-making set was spread out on a table.

"Let's get some beads," said Gracie, bouncing across the room. The beads jiggled on the table. A few rolled onto the floor.

"Want to hear a necklace joke? What did one necklace say to the other?" asked Gracie.

"I don't know. What?" said Allie.

"It said, 'Do you want to hang around together?'" said Gracie.

Allie laughed and started stringing purple beads with silver sparkles. Every once in a while she added a red bead. Gracie's necklace was all green.

When they finished their necklaces, they each made a matching bracelet. Then they stood in front of the mirror.

"Who are those gorgeous gators?" said Gracie.

"They must be movie stars," said Allie. "No, wait! They're us!"

They wore their jewelry while they drank juice and watched a frog singing songs on TV.

"That reminds me, the Rockin' Reptiles concert is coming up," said Allie. "I wish I could go."

"I'm going with my mother. I think she has an extra ticket," said Gracie. "I'll ask if you can come."

"Wow! That would be great," said Allie.

When the TV show was over, Allie went home.

Ring! Ring! That afternoon, the phone rang at Amy's house.

"I'll get it," said Amy, thinking it was Allie. But it was Gracie.

31

"Do you want to come over and bake cookies?" asked Gracie.

"I love baking cookies! Can Allie come, too?" asked Amy.

"I'm only allowed to invite one guest for baking," said Gracie. "We can make catfish cookies."

"Ooh, I like those," said Amy. "I'll be right over!"

Gracie and Amy mixed up a bowl of catfish cookie dough. They took turns spooning the dough onto a cookie sheet.

When they were ready to bake, Gracie's mother came into the kitchen to help them with the oven.

"This batter looks perfect," said Gracie's mother.

"Want to hear a cookie joke? What did one almond cookie say to another?" said Gracie. Without waiting for an answer, she said, "'You're nutty!'"

"You're funny," said Amy, giggling.

When the cookies were done, they each ate two. Then Gracie's mother said, "I have some important work to do now. Can you two play quietly for a while?"

While they played, Gracie turned on her radio very softly. The Rockin' Reptiles' first hit song, "Great Golly Gators," was on the air.

"I wish I could go to the concert Friday night," said Amy.

"My mom and I are going," said Gracie. "Do you want to come with us?"

The minute she said it, she knew it was a mistake. She had only one extra ticket, and she had already asked Allie.

"I'd love to come!" said Amy before Gracie could take it back.

"Um, I can't ask my mom now because she's busy. I'll let you know later," said Gracie, hoping her mother could get another ticket.

"Thanks," said Amy. "I guess I better go now."

"Here, take some cookies," said Gracie. She put some in a bag for Amy.

Amy went next door to her building. As she climbed the steps, she took a cookie out of the bag. She was munching on her cookie when the door opened and Allie stepped out.

"Allie!" said Amy, jumping back.

"Amy!" said Allie, stepping forward. "I was just looking for you." Allie noticed Amy's cookies. "Where'd you get those?"

"I made them with Gracie," said Amy. Amy noticed Allie's jewelry.

"Where'd you get the necklace and bracelet?" she asked.

"I made them with Gracie," said Allie.

"Oh," said Amy. "Gracie sure is fun, isn't she?"

"She sure is," said Allie.

Suddenly they both got very quiet.

I wonder if Amy likes Gracie better than me, thought Allie to herself.

Meantime, Amy was thinking, Does Allie like Gracie better than *me*?

Just then Amy's mother called from the window, "Amy! It's time to come upstairs."

"See you tomorrow," said Allie.

As they headed home, each had a little worried feeling inside. But they tried to forget about it. After all, they had been best friends forever. Nothing could come between them…could it?

5
WHO WILL BE
THE LUCKY GATOR?

The next morning, Allie and Amy met outside their buildings. Allie tied her jump rope to a fence and turned the rope while Amy jumped and chanted,

> *One scaly gator*
> *Jumping on the street,*
> *Left foot. Right foot.*
> *Now both feet!*

While she was jumping, Gracie came by.

"I'll turn the other end," she said, untying the rope from the fence.

As soon as the Gator Girls saw Gracie, their worry came back. Then Amy remembered something. Gracie had invited her to the concert. Allie remembered something, too. Gracie had invited *her* to the concert.

Without thinking, they both blurted out, "Did your mother say I could go with you?"

Allie and Amy looked at each other in amazement. Then they looked at Gracie. Gracie dropped the rope and started bouncing up and down.

"I—I can explain everything," she said.

"You asked *me* to the concert," said Allie, stamping her foot.

"You asked *me* to the concert," said Amy, with her hands on her hips.

"Okay, okay. So I made a teeny tiny little

mistake," said Gracie. She started bouncing even faster. "I was having such a good time with *both* of you that I wanted both of you to come."

"How could we both go when you only had one ticket?" said Allie, getting madder by the minute.

"I didn't think about it right away," said Gracie. "Then I figured my mother could get another ticket."

"Well, can she?" asked Amy in an exasperated voice.

"No, she can't," said Gracie.

"Now what?" said Allie. "Which one of us gets the ticket?"

Gracie looked at Allie, then at Amy, then back to Allie. Her feet were bouncing up and down. Her head was bouncing left and right.

"I can't decide! I like you both. *You* have to decide," said Gracie, flapping her arms.

Allie turned to Amy and said, "I should go because Gracie asked me first."

"She could have asked me first," said Amy. "It doesn't mean she likes you better, you know."

"I know that," said Allie, starting to feel mad at Amy. "But as the saying goes, First to know is the one to go."

"I never heard that before," said Amy.

"Me neither," said Gracie.

"That's because I just made it up," said Allie.

"Then it doesn't count," said Amy, getting mad at Allie.

Whoosh! Marvin whizzed by. He missed Allie's tail by an alligator inch. *Whoosh!* He circled around and whizzed by again, just missing Amy's toes.

The Gator Girls did not say a word.

"What's going on?" asked Marvin. "Why aren't you getting mad at me?"

"We are too busy to worry about an annoying alligator like you," said Amy.

"Now, about that ticket…," began Allie.

"Are you still trying to get tickets to the

concert? Give it up," said Marvin. "They're sold out. Gone. History."

"Not exactly," said Gracie. "I have one extra ticket."

"Oh, really? *One* extra ticket?" said Marvin. "Who will be the lucky gator?"

"It's going to be *me*!" said Allie, looking right at Amy.

"No, it's going to be *me*!" said Amy, looking back.

"Wait!" said Gracie, bouncing faster than

ever. "Don't have a fight! Not because of me."

"Don't worry," said Marvin to Gracie. "They're best friends. They're together-forever goony friends. They *never* fight."

Marvin turned to Allie and Amy. His eyes widened in surprise. The Gator Girls were glaring at each other. Their cool green cheeks had turned hot pink. They were sticking their tongues out at each other.

"I take it back," said Marvin. "The fight has begun!"

6
LOOK WHO'S NOT TALKING

Allie and Amy walked off. Gracie hurried home to see if her mother would try once more to get another ticket. Marvin followed Allie and Amy on his skateboard. He didn't want to miss the Gator Girls' first fight.

"You can't go to the concert without me," Amy said to Allie. "I'll have to sit home alone!"

"But if you go, *I'll* be the one at home!" shouted Allie.

"I'm glad *I* don't have to stay home," said Marvin.

Allie and Amy gave Marvin a dirty look. Then they turned their backs on him.

"I want to hear the Rockin' Reptiles so badly," said Amy.

"Maybe you just want to be with Gracie," said Allie.

"What about you?" said Amy. "You made fancy jewelry with her. Now you're trying to go to the concert with her. Why don't you just be best friends with her?"

"Look who's talking. If I'm not mistaken, you're the one who made cookies with Gracie," said Allie. "I bet you'll eat your cookies at the concert together."

"I bet you'll wear your jewelry at the concert together," said Amy.

"I bet I'm not talking to you anymore!" said Allie.

"I bet I'm not talking to you either!" said Amy.

The Gator Girls turned, put their noses in the air, and stomped off in opposite directions.

Marvin still wanted to follow, but he couldn't go two ways at once. He followed Amy first. He watched her go into the candy store. Then he hurried back to catch up with Allie.

Allie was at the playground, on the swings. She pushed off hard and sailed way up in the air.

"Amy is at the candy store!" called Marvin.

"Amy? Amy who?" Allie called back. "I would give you a message for her— whoever she is—but I am not talking to her."

Hmm, thought Marvin. This could get interesting.

He zipped back to the candy store. Amy was outside, holding a package of swamp-root bubble gum. She was blowing a bubble that covered half her face.

"Your friend Allie is at the playground on the swings," said Marvin.

Pop! Amy's bubble burst.

"I don't have a friend named Allie anymore," she said, pulling gum off her face.

"She says she's not talking to you anyway," said Marvin.

"That goes double for me," said Amy.

Marvin zipped back to the playground. Now Allie was on the monkey bars.

"Amy's chewing swamp-root bubble gum," said Marvin.

"Who cares? I hate that flavor," said Allie.

"By the way, she's not talking to you—double," said Marvin.

"Make that triple for me," said Allie.

Marvin zipped back to the candy store.

"Allie's on the monkey bars now," he said to Amy.

"*Monkey* bars? It figures," said Amy, stuffing three pieces of gum into her mouth at once. She chewed a few times, then said, "Monkey see, monkey do. Allie Gator belongs in the zoo!"

In no time, Marvin was back at the playground, reporting to Allie.

"Amy's chewing three pieces of gum at once," said Marvin.

"Good. Maybe she'll get cavities," said Allie.

"Amy said you belong in the zoo," said
Marvin.

"What did you say? I can't hear you," said
Allie.

Marvin started to repeat what he said.
"Amy said you belong in the—"

"Oh, I heard you. But I don't care. I'm leaving. I have things to do, places to go," said Allie as she started out of the park.

Marvin went back to the candy store one last time to see what Amy was up to. He got there just as Amy's tail was disappearing around the corner.

Thank goodness, thought Marvin. I'm tired of being a goony-bird messenger. I quit!

He skated off in the other direction.

7
THE CRYSTAL
BALL HAS SPOKEN

Allie's head was swimming with questions as she left the park. Did Amy want to be best friends with Gracie? Would she go to the concert and leave Allie behind? Would Allie have to sit home alone for the rest of her life?

Allie walked toward Madame Lulu's Fortune-telling Parlor. If anyone had the answers to her questions, it was Madame Lulu.

When Allie reached Madame Lulu's, she stopped short. The fortune-telling parlor was pink and yellow outside, but it was dark and gloomy inside. She and Amy always went in together. Allie was scared to go in all by herself.

Suddenly she heard a husky voice calling from inside. It was Madame Lulu's voice.

"Greetings, fortune seeker! Come right this way," she ordered.

Clink! Clink! Allie could hear the clink of Madame Lulu's bracelets. Madame Lulu always wore about twenty bracelets on each arm. They clinked together whenever she moved.

Allie was afraid not to obey Madame Lulu. She pushed her way through the beaded curtain.

When Allie's eyes got used to the dark, she noticed that someone was standing next to her. The shape looked familiar. It was…

"Amy!" shouted Allie. "What are you doing here?"

"What are *you* doing here?" Amy shouted back.

"If you are seeking answers, you have come to the right place," said Madame Lulu.

Madame Lulu held out her hand. *Clink!* Amy dropped a dime into her palm. Madame Lulu kept her hand out and looked in Allie's direction. Allie got the hint and gave her a dime, too.

"Please sit down and join hands," said Madame Lulu, slipping the coins into her pocket.

"I'm not holding hands with *her*," huffed Allie.

Madame Lulu closed her eyes and rubbed her head. "I feel anger in the air," she said.

"Ouch! I feel it under the table," said Amy. "She kicked me!"

"I did not!" said Allie.

"Now, now," said Madame Lulu, trying to calm them down.

"No, not now," said Allie. "It happened before! It happened when Amy decided to be best friends with Gracie and not me."

"You're the one who likes Gracie best," said Amy.

"Hold everything!" said Madame Lulu. "Why can't you like Gracie and each other, too?"

"Well, maybe we can," said Allie. "But we can't both go to the concert with her. There's only one ticket."

"Oh, really? What concert is that?" asked Madame Lulu.

"The Rockin' Reptiles," said Amy.

"Oh, I dig them! I mean, I hear they are very good, especially the new drummer," said Madame Lulu, tapping the tabletop.

"We don't know what to do," said Allie.

Madame Lulu gazed into her crystal ball.

"The two of you are going to have to work it out together," said Madame Lulu.

"We can't," said Amy.

"No way!" said Allie.

"You have to," said Madame Lulu. "The crystal ball has spoken!"

But Allie and Amy would not listen. They each crossed their arms and turned away from the other.

Madame Lulu gazed into the crystal ball once more. Tears filled her eyes.

"I see a sad story," she said. "I see two friends who fight. Time goes by. They don't speak to each other. They don't see each other."

"Wait! Is it me and Allie?" asked Amy.

"No. I had a best friend once," said Madame Lulu dreamily. "She was nice. Her name was Glenda.... Or was it Brenda?"

"What happened to her?" asked Allie.

"We had a fight. A very big fight," said Madame Lulu. "And then...and then..."

"Don't tell us you stopped talking to each other! It's too horrible even to think about!" said Amy.

Madame Lulu moaned and threw her head back. She covered her eyes with her hand. *Clink!* She peeked out between her fingers at the Gator Girls.

Allie and Amy looked at each other and gasped. What if the same thing happened to them? What if they really and truly never spoke again? It was definitely too horrible to think about.

The Gator Girls jumped up.

"We have to go now," said Allie.

"We have things to work out," said Amy.

They dashed out of the fortune-telling parlor.

"Thank you, Madame Lulu!" they called over their shoulders.

Madame Lulu smiled and waited. As soon as she saw the Gator Girls turn the corner, she picked up the phone and dialed her best friend's number.

"Hello, Brenda?" said Madame Lulu, grinning. "Remember that fight we had when we were kids, and we didn't speak for three whole hours? Well, I just told two best friends the story. Of course, I exaggerated a little...."

8
WHAT TO DO?

On their way home, Allie and Amy walked through the park. They were passing the dock at Gator Pond when a big alligator waved hello. It was Bart, who rented the boats.

"Are you taking a boat out today?" he called.

"We can't. We have thinking to do," said Allie.

"A boat's the best place for thinking," said Bart. "It's nice and quiet."

The next thing they knew, they were rowing around in the middle of the pond, talking over their problem.

"Three of us want to go to the concert. But one of us has to stay home. The question is who," said Amy.

"I've got it. Gracie!" said Allie.

"Be nice," said Amy. "It's *her* ticket."

"Yeah, I guess that wouldn't be fair," said Allie. "That leaves the two of us. How can we make two into one?"

"This is no time for math riddles!" said Amy, fumbling with her oar. It slipped out of its holder and—*splash!*—fell into the water.

"Uh-oh, oar overboard!" yelled Allie.

Amy fished around and grabbed the oar.

"Wait! This time I've got a genius plan, and I mean it!" said Allie. "We can make a costume—"

"Why? It isn't Halloween," said Amy.

"No, no. It can be one *big* costume that two of us can fit in," said Allie. "We'll look like one gator, and we'll only need one ticket."

"Yay! That's it!" shouted Amy. "You *are* a genius!"

They were so excited they both dropped their oars in the water.

"Two oars overboard!" yelled Allie. They fished the oars out and put them back in the oarlocks.

"Uh-oh," said Amy. "I just thought of something. The two of us could fit in one costume, but we couldn't fit in one seat."

"Oh, that's right," said Allie, disappointed. "I guess I'm not a genius."

"Let's put our heads together," said Amy. "I've heard that helps."

Allie and Amy touched foreheads and closed their eyes. They waited for something to come to them. Suddenly something did.

Crash! Bam! Another boat smashed right into the Gator Girls' boat.

"Gracie! What are you doing here?" asked Amy as their boat rocked wildly.

"I saw you two out here, and I wanted to tell you something," said Gracie, her oars bouncing up and down. "I tried really hard to get another ticket to the concert, but I couldn't do it."

"We haven't come up with anything yet either," said Allie.

"Let's put our heads together again," said Amy. "If two heads are better than one, then three heads must be better than two."

Gracie leaned out from her boat, and the three gators put their heads together and closed their eyes.

"Two gators, one ticket. What to do?" said Allie, thinking out loud.

"Not another math riddle," said Amy.

"Did you say riddles? You know I love riddles!" shouted Gracie, lifting her head. "And I'm good at math, too. We just have to divide. We take one concert and divide it by two. Allie goes to the first half. Amy goes to the second half."

"Wow! That's it! You're a math genius!" shouted Allie.

They were so excited they did something they were never supposed to do. They jumped up and down in the boat. Gracie fell in first.

"Alligator overboard!" Allie yelled, jumping in after Gracie.

"Two alligators overboard!" Amy yelled, jumping in after Allie.

"Three alligators overboard!" yelled Gracie, Allie, and Amy together as they splashed and giggled in the pond.

Vrooom! Bart came speeding up in his motorboat. "You know the rules. No swimming allowed," he said.

"We're sorry. We just got excited because all three of us are going to the Rockin' Reptiles concert," said Amy, treading water.

"Make that four. I'll be there, too," said Bart.

He helped the girls into the motorboat. He tied their rowboats to the back while they wrung out their clothes and Allie dried off her glasses. The girls were excited. A motorboat ride was going to be fun!

Vrooom! Bart started back to the dock, doing a few fancy turns for the three friends on the way.

They thanked Bart when they got back to the dock. Then Gracie looked at her watch.

"Oops! I'm late," she said. "I'm going shopping with my mother. See you tonight, gators!"

Allie and Amy watched her bounce away.

"I love Gracie's genius plan, don't you?"

said Amy. "It's so great. We'll both get to hear the Reptiles."

"I still wish we could be there at the same time," said Allie.

"Yes, but this is better than not going at all," said Amy.

"I guess so," agreed Allie. "Do you want to come to my house now for lemonade?"

"Sure," said Amy. And they skipped all the way to Allie's building.

9
ROCKIN' REPTILES!

Ring! Ring! The phone rang at Allie's house.

"Who can that be?" Allie said to Amy. "It can't be you, because you're here. And it can't be Gracie, because she's shopping."

Ring! Ring! The phone rang again.

"If you want to find out who it is, why don't you answer it?" said Amy.

"Good idea," said Allie, picking up the phone.

"Hello," said a husky voice at the other end.

"Madame Lulu? Is that you?" asked Allie in amazement. Madame Lulu had never called before!

Amy started hopping from one foot to the other. "It's Madame Lulu? What does she want?" she asked.

"Shh. I can't hear her when you're talking," said Allie.

"What's she saying?" whispered Amy.

Allie listened carefully. Then she dropped the phone and grabbed Amy's hand. "She got us another ticket!"

The Gator Girls jumped up and down, then danced around in a circle, singing the Rockin' Reptiles song "No More Crocodile Tears for Me!"

"Hello? Hello!" called Madame Lulu's voice from the floor.

"Oops! We forgot all about Madame Lulu," said Amy.

Allie picked up the phone again.

"Thank you very much for the ticket," she said, remembering her manners. "How did you manage to get one?"

"Fortune-tellers have their ways," said Madame Lulu mysteriously.

"Will you be at the concert, too?" asked Amy.

"I'll be there," said Madame Lulu, and she hung up the phone.

Allie and Amy met Gracie and her mother in front of Gator Palace at seven-thirty. Allie had on her necklace. Amy was wearing the matching bracelet. Gracie wore a GRACIE T-shirt with a big Rockin' Reptiles button pinned on. All three girls were waving Rockin' Reptiles flags.

When they went inside, the palace was buzzing with excitement. They followed Gracie's mother down the aisle.

The lights were starting to dim as Allie and Amy slipped into their row. Allie felt something under her foot. It felt like another foot.

"Ouch!" cried a voice. It was a goony voice. A whiny voice. It was...

"MARVIN!!!" cried Allie. "Watch where you put your feet!"

"Watch where I put my *feet*? Watch where you're *stepping*!" said Marvin. "Hey, what are you two doing here, anyway? I thought there was only one ticket."

"Isn't it amazing what intelligent alligators can do?" piped in Amy.

"I don't think Marvin knows about that," said Allie.

A big alligator waved from across the aisle. It was Bart. The girls waved back. They looked around for Madame Lulu, but they didn't see her in the audience.

Just then Gator Palace grew dark, and the curtain went up. There were the Rockin' Reptiles live, onstage! There was a moment of silence before a guitar started playing a wild and crazy song.

The keyboard joined in, and the drums beat out an awesome rhythm. *Bam, bam. Clink! Bam, bedoo-bop bam. Clink! Clink!*

Allie and Amy looked at each other. It wasn't possible!

They looked at the drummer. She had about twenty bracelets on each arm. It *was* possible. The new Rockin' Reptiles drummer was Madame Lulu! They caught her eye and waved. Madame Lulu waved a drumstick back at them.

"So that's how she got the ticket," said Amy. "She knew someone in the band."

"That's right. Herself," said Allie.

Bam, bam. Bam, bedoo-bop bam. Clink!

"Everyone sing along," the lead Reptile said into the microphone.

That was just what the gators were waiting to hear. They jumped up from their seats and started singing,

> *We're Rockin' Reptiles*
> *In the swamp.*
> *Everybody sing,*
> *Everybody stomp!*

"This is so cool!" said Amy, squeezing Allie's hand.

"I can hardly believe we're here," said Allie, squeezing back.

They went back to singing.

We like to rock,
We like to swing!
Everybody dance,
Everybody sing!

Marvin danced in the aisle. Gracie bounced in her seat. And Allie and Amy tapped their tails together all night long.